BANYAN

by

Cynthia A. Williams

ACKNOWLEDGEMENTS

My thanks to Carol Rooksby Weidlich, Director ~ Webmaster ~ Newsletter Editor, Friends of the Fort Myers Library, who passed my request for a photo of Lorelei to Carolyn Ford, Friends of the Fort Myers Library, who found the photo I remembered seeing in Prudy Taylor Board's *Pages from the Past* and emailed it to me and then actually *went to see* Helen Farrell at the Southwest Florida Museum of History to ask for more photos. Thank you, Helen, for sending me three images to choose from and for offering your assistance in sizing them appropriately. The image of Lorelei that these wonderful women have provided will grace the back cover of the printed copies of *BANYAN*.

The image for the front cover is the skilled photography of Bernard W. Moore, who captured in his photo of a Banyan tree the mood and very essence of this mystery.

PREFACE

I read that a preface is supposed to tell the reader where the idea for the novel in hand came from. I have no idea where *BANYAN* came from. Its origin is as mysterious as the story itself. The opening sentences came to me whole, I wrote them down, and then it was very nearly automatic writing. Honestly, I suspect that it is a meld of events and relationships experienced in both present and past lives. Memory flows like a river through time, picking up and discarding debris, and this debris of memory, floating wholly or partially submerged in one's unconscious, may, in both waking and sleeping dreams, emerge suddenly as a story with fully fleshed people walking around and talking and all you can do is write as fast as you can to keep up with them.

Any events and characters in *BANYAN* are pure fiction, of course, with the exception of the statue of Lorelei. She is real. Today, you will find her in the Berne Davis Gardens in Fort Myers, but decades ago, when the estate to which she belonged was sold off for an apartment complex, she was given to the Fort Myers library, and her subsequent public exposure cost her her head. She has been decapitated.

The setting for *BANYAN* is the famous Burroughs House in Ft. Myers. It is a national historic site, and the setting today for weddings and other lavish private and civic affairs.

The Cuvier family is a figment of my imagination. Or the puzzle pieces of personalities and experiences in other lives, fitted together into a new story that we shall call fiction.

DEDICATION

With gratitude and love to my steadfast, merry and long-suffering Bear. He is forever patient, forever there for me, forever my best friend.

INTRODUCTION

The Banyan tree is an ancient East Indian fig tree. It drops vines laterally from its limbs and the vines take root, growing decade by decade into multiple trunks that merge gradually with one another and with the mother trunk. In this way, the tree travels from its center, its thickening vines serpentine, its roots like monstrous, writhing anacondas. It is an alarming phenomenon.

A mind functions similarly.

That summer lasted so long. The summer after Father killed himself. Hot, my God. We thought it would never end. Mornings we awoke to darkness and thunder. The thunder rolled over upon us, enclosed us. The house vibrated with it. We sat in the parlor with the lamps lit and sweated as the thunder rolled over and shook the house.

I gazed often at my brother that summer. His face was disintegrating. He had been a beautiful boy and a handsome young man but the face I saw that summer was aged and wan, the eyes vacuous. I decided that I was tired of him.

My visions also began that summer, visions of rooms in houses I had never been in. I had been born in this house and had slept in it every night of my life and I would die in it. I was resigned to that now. But I had these glimpses of rooms in other houses. They passed across my inner vision without apparent connection to anything I might be doing at the time. I liked it when this happened. I thought these illusive fragments of apparently someone else's memory strange and wonderful. They excited me.

My brother would ask, "What are you smiling at?" and I would reply truthfully and with awestruck happiness, "I don't know."

Gerry probably thought my mind was slipping, that his spinster sister was beginning to dodder mentally. He undoubtedly imagined that my firm, middle-aged tread was beginning to falter and that when I stepped at last into fragile old age my mind would take flight altogether and I would begin to creep daintily about, whispering and nodding and smiling. But who knows what he thought. He slurped his coffee and stared out the kitchen window, his eyes glazed over with his own inner visions, and I knew that he didn't care anymore. Much less, in fact, than I did, and that he undoubtedly never had.

Gerry had given up, long ago. Had resigned himself, as I had. Though at times I glimpsed a menacing, an almost calculating look in his eyes. Like a man cornered and without a ghost of chance who might yet make a dash for it. It worried me, when I saw that look in his eyes. That he might try. Because I was sure that if he did he would be lost forever. Puttering around the kitchen, glancing occasionally at Gerry as he stood staring silently out the window, drinking his coffee from gleaming English bone china, I thought of some grass shack in the Amazon and of my brother, lying in a dark corner of it, his cheek pressed in Macaw shit, lizards darting up his arms. If I had described these fantasies to Gerry he would have laughed, we both would have, and agreed that I'd read too much Conrad. But then I would have seen in his eyes a quickening of interest, a consideration of possibilities. In Gerry I had always sensed an undercurrent capacity for destructiveness, even for violence, certainly for abandonment. So I did not tell him. I didn't talk to him anymore about much of anything. Clearly, he wasn't interested in anything I had to say.

One of my visions is of a bedroom on the second floor of a house in what seems to be a wilderness setting. Outside the windows, Spanish moss, lifting lightly in a breeze, trails from the limbs of old oaks. Between the two windows, a girl is sitting at a dressing table. She is gazing out the window to her left at a skimpy front lawn with an elliptical, sandy drive. That is all. I don't know what period of time it is; I can't tell what the girl is wearing. I only sense that it is a long time ago. Another era. I do have the impression that the house and grounds are run down, that they may have been grand once, but are now rather seedy. I also have the impression that the girl is waiting for someone. Watching the drive for someone's arrival.

Even before Father died, Gerry and I seldom left the house. Gerry ordered our groceries over the telephone. Once or twice a year he walked into town to consult with our attorney or the banker. Occasionally, for a little outing, he walked into town to the drugstore. He liked the bright merchandise, the smells of the lotions and creams and suntan oils, the dusting powders, and new plastic. Occasionally he came home with something in a little brown paper sack and took it upstairs without showing me what it was. I guess he was stashing things away up there. I was too honorable to investigate when he was out, though once I did glimpse, in passing his room, one of his purchases. A shiny new red and yellow tin sand pail sat on his bedside table. It was painted with pictures of beach balls and small boys and girls chunking sand into little sand pails with tiny red shovels. Drawn irresistibly into the room, I peeked and saw that he had put in it some of our old oyster shells that we used to gather from the riverbed at low tide. It had simply not occurred to me that Gerry might be buying toys.

On at least one occasion that I can remember, he came home with something for me. He had left the house under lowering, darkening clouds. I said to him at the door that he should take his raincoat but he just went on down the side steps that led off the kitchen and let the door practically close in my face. It made me mad.

The rain had slackened when I saw him coming home about two hours later. He was holding his khaki jacket, spotted with the few light drops that were still falling, clutched protectively over a small brown paper sack that he held against his chest. Head lowered, he pushed through the gate of our white picket fence. When he reached the top step I opened the door and stepped back to let him in. Gerry lifted his head and stopped in the open doorway, staring at me. And I knew that in that instant he did not know who I was. I had never before, nor have I ever since, seen the sweet serenity I saw then on my brother's face, in his eyes in the instant that he lifted his face to mine, in the instant before, seeing me standing there, his eyes began to cloud, first with confusion, and then with pain. He dropped his head and pulled the package from under his jacket and looked at it with a frown. Then abruptly he thrust it at me.

"Here. I got you something."

He stepped past me, shrugging off his wet jacket, and I closed the door, staring at the sack I held. Then I reached in and pulled out a box of dusting powder and Gerry turned and looked at me. The box was small, oval, the beige paper sprinkled with pale pink flowers around the face of a sort of Marie Antoinette portrait. When I lifted my eyes to Gerry's, in wonder and gratitude, he looked away, ashamed. He shrugged.

"I don't know," he said. "Made me think of your birthday parties when we were kids. Your presents smelled like that."

Gerry had an artist's eye for color and design. As a child he had liked Mother's bottles of pink and lilac-colored colognes, the pretty labels on them. He would reach up and take a bottle down from her dressing table and shake it to make the cologne water bubble and sparkle. Standing in his little shorts and knee high socks and white shoes, frowning, furiously shaking the bottle. Mother would sit there smiling at him, reaching tentatively for the bottle, afraid he would lose his grip and smash it on the floor.

"Thank you, Gerry. It's nice to have a present."

He turned away, almost angrily.

We lived in a very grand house hidden almost entirely from view by a jungle of palms and exotic trees imported from Africa, Egypt and the Orient. Flowering and fruit trees were all in a tangle, hibiscus and gardenias, bougainvillea and magnolias dropping spent blossoms upon decomposing scraps of lemons, limes, kumquats and avocados. When Father ceased to care, we did, too. It all just got to be too much for him. And then, too, the expense of keeping the gardeners must finally have seemed pointless to him. An exercise in futility. Like everything else.

Our property extended 450 feet along the bank of the shimmering Caloosa River. In the old days paddle wheelers used to come up the river from the Gulf of Mexico carrying passengers, store goods and mail to what was then a clean, quiet, pretty little town fourteen miles upriver from the glistening shell beaches of Florida's southwest coast. But that was a long time ago. Now people arrived by airplane. Once in a while I would hear one overhead. Every single time I would think it was thunder. I'd look up from my reading and say, "Is it going to rain?" and Gerry would just roll his eyes.

I always liked the river. Sometimes I would peer at it through the dirty panes of the French doors that had once opened onto our back porch. Now and then I would see a shrimp boat heading out to the Gulf.

After the police and the reporter and the coroner left and the undertaker had had Father's body carried out the front door and down the high front steps that flowed like a woman's tiered gown from our veranda, I had closed the front door and locked it.

I did not understand why that old man had done it. He had become quite feeble, his skeletal hand trembling when he lifted a spoon to his mouth. For years he had been little more than a ghost in the house, keeping to the upper floors, as if he were afraid to intrude upon the living. Keeping in the shadows, visibly wincing at daylight. But so far as we knew he was not in pain. He was not diseased. He seemed all right in his head— just a little remote. He had been withdrawing from the living for years. But that seemed natural enough. I cannot think why, then, when Gerry came down the stairs and told me what he had found up there, why I felt a thrilling surge of triumph, of vindication. Of pure and simple satisfaction. Followed immediately by anger.

My initial emotional reaction stunned me.

I wanted to talk to Gerry about it. But I knew he absolutely would not speak of it. He had come down the stairs that day from the little play room with the dormer window on the third floor, his face white. He was holding tightly to the banister as he came down because his knees were trembling. He could hardly stand. I thought he was going to vomit.

I have never known where our mother and father came from. I don't know anything about their families. I don't know who our grandparents were. By the time I was old enough to ask, I knew by some instinct that they did not want to be questioned about the past. I don't know why. I only know that they had all the money in the world and nothing to do but play. I know they were passionately in love. Always, always. In the 32 years he lived after Mother died, Father never had so much as a friendship with another woman.

But they were wild about him. Every woman who ever so much as glanced at him. Even as kids, Gerry and I would giggle behind our hands at the looks on their faces when they first saw him. He was astonishing. Sometimes you could hear the sharp intake of breath when a woman turned and saw him coming toward her. But he was not interested in them.

Father was a gentleman. Impeccably groomed, exquisitely tailored. A gracious, generous and attentive host. And in company with others, always laughing. He was wonderful. Gerry and I loved him so much we couldn't get enough of him into our eyes, couldn't touch him enough. I think it was the same day that they carried the body of the old man out of the house that I said to Gerry, "I loved him too much." Gerry was so angry he couldn't speak. Had to leave the room. I watched him go in bewilderment, my heart gone right out of my body.

One morning after spitting toothpaste out of my mouth, I looked at myself in the mirror and thought, "You never loved him at all. You didn't even like him. These last years, you almost hated him. Why?"

He gave us this great house, and a trust, with lawyers to administer it. But he lived with a deep and voiceless fury in him that showed in his eyes every time he happened to glance at either one of us. He made every effort for the last decades of his life not even to look at us. He'd sit up in his room listening to the radio and gazing out the window, and if I tapped on the doorframe and cautiously entered the room, he would not turn to acknowledge my presence. On the one hand I thought he was too old and stiff to turn, that it would have been a painful hardship on him to have to. On the other hand, I thought he was just stubbornly determined to ignore me. As if he were punishing me for something.

But I never knew I was angry until he died. When I saw Gerry at the foot of the stairs, white around the mouth, his legs giving at the knees, a fury swept through me such as I had never felt in my life. It rocked me. I hated that old man then. I hated him enough to kill him.

The fury swept through me and was gone. Leaving a certain amount of devastation. The litter after the storm. For the rest of the summer I was picking up the pieces. Trying to put back together whatever it was that was broken.

It was a hellish summer. Hotter than any I ever remember. The only relief came every afternoon about 3:00 when a current of air would pass through the room and we'd hear a distant roll of thunder, soon followed by the *whsssh* of our afternoon rain shower, the silvery curtain of rain sparkling in the sunlight and misting through the window screen into the room. Then I'd get up from the sofa and stand before the window, inhaling deeply the hot, metallic scent of the rain on the wires of the screen, letting the mist of rain moisten my face. After about an hour, the thunder would begin to diminish in the distance and the rain would slacken and suddenly stop. Then the street outside and the jungle foliage around the house would steam in the sunshine, and the air in the house grow so oppressively heavy that I would feel as if I were drowning. I would fall back into my chair, rubbing an ice cube up and down my arms and neck, letting the water drip off my fingertips and trickle down the cleavage of my breasts.

We might have thrown open the French doors to our back veranda but they had been closed and locked for years and I guess neither of us really wanted to risk exposing ourselves.

All of the windows in the rooms we lived in were left open and the dust-laden curtains drawn back all the time, but the Frangipani and rubber plant trees and vines kept the ground floor of the house in absolute gloom and gave us the privacy we needed. We lived almost entirely in the back parlor where so much of the life in that house, when there had been life in the house, had been lived. It had been our parents' big party room, but now it was a library and sitting room. Two deep, soft, shabby armchairs faced each other across a broad, low table where I tossed unfinished books and Gerry dropped the newspapers and magazines he brought home from the barbershop. On one side of the coffee table against the wall was a comfortable old sofa. I had made slipcovers for the sofa and chairs when the original upholstery had worn clear through to the stuffing. Now the slipcovers were dark and threadbare from use, and always rumpled and dragged down on one side or the other. I had never been much of a housekeeper. I just never cared. I think Gerry would have liked a spit and polish sort of environment, but he wasn't going to get it from me and he knew it. So he just lived with it.

Along the one interior wall of the room were floor-to-ceiling bookshelves. Father's vast library. Every room in the house had books packed into shelves or stacked on the furniture, but this room held the important books. I had read all of them I wanted to. Now and then I picked something off one of the shelves and started reading but after a while I'd put it back, or simply drop it on any chair or table in the room. Father would have been appalled. But nothing in these books could sustain my interest anymore. They could not divert my attention from what was going on in my own head, the unfolding, petal by petal, of my own strange new inner life.

The girl at the window, waiting. The meaning of her whole existence seems to be that she is waiting for somebody who will never come. I was certain of that. That he would never come.

All the while I was going about my daily life that summer, in the back of my head she was sitting there, staring out the window at that white sandy drive and the fountain in the center of it, hot and empty in the sun.

Once, for one paralyzed moment of wonder, I heard her breathing. And I felt the weight of a silk dress, heavy with cold beadwork, against small, bare breasts.

I awoke on the twenty-ninth of August to the sound of thunder. I lay listening to the rumbling, feeling the big old house tremble with it. Then with a flash of lightening and terrifying crash of thunder, rain flung itself against my window screen, splattering the floor below. I jumped up and brought down the window hard and the rain rushed against the glass. Ankles stiff, I limped into the bathroom and yanked on the overhead light. The house had been wired for electricity in 1905. The electric cords, in a cavalier display of affluence, had been left fashionably visible on the walls. They were looped from the ceilings to the light fixtures and electric fans on tables in the dining room, the kitchen, the bedrooms. The light in my bathroom was still a naked bulb suspended from the ceiling. It was ugly. No longer a sign of wealth and modernity, but of antiquity. We were living in a museum. The light made the big, high-ceilinged room yellow. I started water running in my old claw-footed bathtub and the sound of the water running into the tub joined the sound of the rain on the roof until I could not tell them apart. The steam rising from the tub filled the room and as I turned off the faucets with a squeak and lay back in the hot water, I felt as if I were in a candlelit cave in a cold, wet forest. The room smelled of Sweetheart soap.

The rain drummed on the roof. Thunder rolled, lightening crashed, and the light bulb hanging from the ceiling danced a bit on its cord. I closed my eyes.

I may have dozed for a moment. Then I "came to" with a start. It had happened again. My eyes were open but I was gazing with wonder at the place I had just been in. A bedroom on the upper floor of an abandoned house. The old, channeled wood floor was bare. Curled, brittle strips of century-old wallpaper hung from the exposed wallboards. The only furnishings in the room were the bed and a bureau against the wall. Through a large window to the right of the bed I saw a great oak tree, the heavy limbs dragging Spanish moss. The sky was dreary, sodden with the moisture of a spent rainstorm. I have the sense that all the downstairs rooms were empty but for a couple of Negroes hanging about. Caretakers. No. Jailors. To the old woman bound up in a sheet on the bed. The sheet is thin, grey with age, yellowed, too, with old urine. They bring her a little food once a day. Leave water. She is grey as ash, like a cold, charred stick of wood. I know that the Negro women living downstairs are waiting for her to die.

I lay in the tub, trying to see clearly into this fading room, but I could only peer back into it through a clouded consciousness. It was like waking from a dream and trying to go back to sleep and have the dream continue. The water in the tub grew tepid, then cold. When I sat up to run more hot water, I felt chilled. Reluctantly, I pulled the plug in the tub.

When I had dressed and gone downstairs, the house was still quite dark. The storm had spent itself, leaving only a little rain falling lightly, and the steady dripping from the trees. I flipped on a dim light in the kitchen and saw that it was only seven. Gerry would be sleeping still. I put on water for tea. Through the open windows, the rain pat-patted the rotting wood of the old windowsills. The white paint on them was peeling, the wood soft underneath. A light breeze blew a few drops of the rain onto the chipped porcelain drain board and sink below the windows. I could hear the rain plashing through those big elephant ear leaves outside. I stood lost in thought, gazing at the water bubbling in my teakettle on the stove, and I didn't hear Gerry come into the kitchen. I jumped when suddenly he was there beside me, reaching up into the cabinet above the counter for a cup and saucer, reaching flat-footed where I had had to stand on tip toe. He was in his pajamas and a rag of a bathrobe, loosely belted. I had hated that bathrobe when it was new, the swirls of dark, ugly colors. Daddy had given it to him for Christmas one year. Now it was so old and worn that even freshly washed, it looked dirty. Gerry absolutely would not let me throw it away.

"Good morning," I said.

"Morning."

I steeped my tea bags and Gerry spooned coffee into the strainer of his coffee pot.

Neatly wiping coffee grains with the edge of his hand into the sink, Gerry set his coffee pot on the stove, turned on the burner and went to the door for his newspaper. The side door off the kitchen was the only door to the outside that either of us ever opened. High, narrow, concrete steps led down from it to a short walk to the gate in the white picket fence surrounding our property. When Gerry opened the door and leaned over to pick his wet newspaper off the stoop, I could hear cars pulling into and out of the filling station across the street. It was a red and white Texaco station and when cars pulled in and out some cable they ran over made a bell go *clang-clang*. I'd hear it sometimes late at night. It was startling to be reminded that there was another world, filled with busy people, right out there just on the other side of our trees, of our absurd little picket fence.

Sometimes fragments of music drifted from the cars as they waited for the light to change at the intersection out front. Each time I'd tilt my head toward the open window to catch the tune. *"I want you, I need you, I-I lu-u-uve you, with all my hear-ar-ar-ar-ar-ar -art."* Then the noise of a hot rod, stripped of its muffler, roaring away.

I smiled. The vision I had had in my bath had made me happy. I turned on the radio. Peggy Lee.

Tra la la, twiddle dee dee dee

It gives me a thrill,

To wake up in the morning

To the mockin'bird's trill.

Gerry carefully unfolded his soaked and heavy paper to the front page, then turned to watch his coffee pot. Sipping my tea, I edged over to the newspaper and glanced down at the picture on the front page. The headline was huge.

BROTHER, SISTER SUFFOCATE IN ABANDONED ICE BOX

The photograph accompanying this headline was of the stripped interior of a small, old-fashioned refrigerator, the kind with the condenser on top. The door was sagging open and even in the clouded newspaper photo, the indentations in it were obvious. The lower half of the door had been kicked almost completely out. It was hard to imagine that the heels of that little girl's shoes could have nearly beaten a hole in that door. They speculated that the boy, being younger, had died first. That it may have taken about twenty minutes for both of them to die. She had almost kicked through the door when she gave out.

I closed my eyes and stood rocking slightly from my heels to the balls of my feet. I felt as if my head were circling, circling the icebox rocking, the muffled screams. My heart looped and a cold rage swept through me.

Tra la la, twiddle dee dee dee

It gives me a thrill,

To wake up in the morning

To the mockin'bird's trill.

My hands began to shake so badly that my cup was jerking all over the saucer.

Tra la la, twiddle dee dee dee

There's peace and good will,

Gerry turned quickly. "What is it? What's the matter?"

I felt as if I were going to shatter. I have seen glass shatter into pieces fine as shaved ice, feathery fine as snow.

Gerry moved quickly, shoving me aside from the counter with his elbow. He snatched up the paper and locked it closed under his arm in one movement.

My body was jerking as if I were being hit.

When it's late in the evening I climb up the hill

And survey all my kingdom while everything's still.

Only me and the sky and an ol'whippoorwill

Singin' songs in the twilight on Mockin'Bird Hill.

I threw both hands over my ears, screaming, *"Turn it off."*

Furiously Gerry switched off the radio then grabbed me in his arms, held my head tight against his chest. "I'm here, Clar. We're all right. We're all right. Remember how sometimes you have bad dreams? That's all it was. Just one of those lousy dreams."

But something had moved in me at the sight of that photograph. It had come at me with a huge and violent movement, like a beast out of the dark. It had shaken me more violently than anything in my life.

I was confused all day. I couldn't focus on what was bothering me. The kids in the icebox. The woman dying alone in that decaying house. I was not interested when, later that morning, Gerry informed me that a tropical depression was forming 150 miles off the coast of Cuba. Good, was all I thought. Maybe it will blow this damn house away.

The sun was in and out all day. In the afternoon, as I walked across the front of the house on the second floor, I happened to glance through the glass of the double French doors that opened there onto a railed porch, a second floor balcony in the center of the house. I saw a little dark-haired girl in a brown dress standing on the sidewalk just on the other side of our front gate.

She was looking up at the house. From her position she could not have seen more than the long walk leading up to our front steps and the widow's walk on top of the house. Perhaps the dormer window of the playroom on the third floor. The room where father put the muzzle of a gun precisely over the center of his heart. The sunshine was brilliant, the sky filled with big, white, wind-driven clouds, and our pale yellow and white house must have been very bright in her eyes. She was frowning up at the house and if I didn't know better, I would have sworn she was looking directly at me. She stood there for a moment, and then she went on. I wondered what could possibly have interested a child in our big old house. Not that it wasn't beautiful. It was splendid indeed.

"*SPLENDID*," Father said, amused by the word. "Perfectly *splendid*, ole boy, old sport." He twirled an invisible mustache. Gerry and I stood before him, grinning. Giving a twirl of an imaginary walking stick, he swaggered up and down the veranda.

"Gerald, the neighbors will see you," Mother said and started to giggle.

"Ole boy, old sport, ole ring-a-ding capital fellow."

"Gerald, *stop it*." Mother's laughter was like the ringing of crystal bells. Her throat, like her wrists, her limbs, were long and slender and white.

I'd hear them sometimes, laughing in other rooms. They were like two big kids at play all the time. I have a vague, early memory of Father taking Mother's delicate face in his hands and planting little kisses, soft as raindrops all over it, murmuring "Darling, darling, darling." I loved them both so much my heart hurt with love.

I don't think they should have put the picture of that beaten icebox in the newspaper. The photo was obscene.

The next day it rained and rained. The tropical depression hadn't been given the status of a storm yet, so they hadn't named it. But it was building. All afternoon we sat in the lamp-lit parlor, limp-wristed, glistening, weighted down by the heat and humidity. We listened to the rain dripping from the eaves of the house, dripping from the leaves of the trees and the bladed tips of the palm fronds, splattering the bruised and broken hibiscus blossoms that littered the muddy grounds and walkways around the house. We could hear the mosquitoes outside starting up after each rain. In the steaming jungle outside the windows, they swarmed in dark clouds. And always the hot rods of the kids blasting away from the intersection, radios trailing snatches of song. *"Blue, blue, blue suede shoes...."*

After each rain, in moments when the street outside was quiet, we could hear the cars rushing across the bridge that spanned the mile-wide river behind the house, the cars making great water wings of spray that arched and fell over the concrete sides of the bridge and made a regular, almost rhythmic sheeting sound.

We still thought of the bridge as new, though it was now over three decades old. When we were kids, the paved street that now ran past our house to the bridge had been a dirt footpath to the riverbank where Gerry and I poked oyster shells out of the muck with sticks. We thought that the swirl of cream and purple inside the shells was melted pearl. They were our secret, hidden treasure.

Up until the twenties, we had had a boat dock out back. When Gerry and I were children, weekend houseguests sometimes came in sleek, teakwood motor-boats and tied up to the dock. Our parents had parties nearly every weekend in those days. From offshore in that long ago world, our house must have looked like a hotel, filled with lights and music and laughter, the young, expensively dressed men and women coming and going in their boats and motor cars night and day.

After Mother died, Father stood sometimes at twilight on the dock, gazing out over the river. Then when they started building the bridge, he'd go out there during the day to watch the construction. His world had changed. It was gone.

Out of nowhere, nothing, I'd see the kids in the icebox again, sweat-soaked, screaming.

I don't think anybody in town paid any attention when Father died. I think everybody he had ever known in that town was dead.

Gerald Chamblis Cuvier the Fifth and his beautiful bride Sayre arrived in Las Palmas on the impossibly bright morning of October 10, 1900. They came up the river by steamboat and when Sayre saw her house slowly emerging from the riverfront, she clasped her hands together and cried, "*Ohhhh...*" her eyes sparkling like the splinters of light on the river water. The sun was so brilliant on the river it watered the eyes of the crowd gathered on shore, so that their first glimpse of Mother was a shimmering brightness of pink and white gossamer lifting and floating in the wind.

Waiting to greet Gerald Cuvier and his bride were Gerald's lawyer, the broker who had sold Gerald the house, the minister with a delegation from the local Episcopal church, and a ladies society, a welcoming committee of the town's social elite. The long dresses of the ladies were lashing in the wind. They held their big hats on, feathers whipping, with both hands, their eyes frantic for a first glimpse of the face, the form, the dress of my mother. They had already met *him*. They could scarcely look at him without their cheeks warming. Now they wanted to see the woman who could legally claim him. Who shared this god's bed. Women too proud to come were waiting anxiously at home for the first reports to come in from the welcoming committee. Was she beautiful? Was her dress simply beyond cost? Was she proud? This exceedingly young man had come to town and bought a Georgian-Revival masterpiece, perfect, splendid beyond description, sitting like a toy house in an enormous flowering garden on the bank of a shining river and then he had gone back to whatever mysterious place he came from, and brought his bride to her new home.

Sayre looked up at her husband with the whole glory of the house in her eyes, and from the overwhelming fullness of his heart he threw back his head and gave to all the assembled curious his rich, deep, joyous laughter. Any other man, giving so open and spontaneous an expression of his love and delight, they would have thought lacking in taste and refinement. But he was perfect. He was larger than the house, larger than their world. He had brought a new world with him and its center would be that magnificent house.

The entire entourage followed Mother and Father to the house, the young couple walking in the lead, Father by the gentle pressure of his arm reining her in, keeping her from lifting her skirts and running. The crowd hung back at the gate until Father, turning with a grin and a broad sweep of his arm, motioned them in. They swarmed into the house, the women, encouraged by mother's easy and friendly way and on the swell of her own energy and excitement, hurrying with her up the stairs to inspect her new home. The chattering and laughter that filled the house on that day remained a continuing part of its life for the next nine years. And the women who were with her on that shining day loved her from then until the day she died. That is why, in hindsight, I could not understand why so few people came to her funeral.

It was always my impression that Father bought the house on impulse. For fun. For Mother. I think he was a rover. I think he might easily have boarded another boat one day with Mother and sailed away if he had taken the notion. But once I came, I guess Father's sailing days were over. I don't think he minded.

When Mother was big with me, soon after they moved in, she remodeled a large room on the second floor for a nursery, filling it with Flemish lace and arranging on the white wicker furniture a bright silver baby cup, rattle, teething ring, comb and brush. A little white leather Bible, the cover soft as doeskin. The whole room was white as milk. I'm sure that the first sight my eyes ever beheld in this world was of their young, shining, incredibly beautiful faces leaning over my crib, grinning at their new toy. My guardian angels incarnate. Dimly I remember white lace, sunlight, the tinkling of glass wind chimes.

Mother wore a fragrance that carried after it the faintest scent of tangerine.

Do you ever think about Mother?" I asked Gerry one evening that summer.

"No."

They named the tropical storm Estelle. The river was running fast now by the sea wall, overlapping it, swift, dark, white-capped. I liked it. I wanted to go out and stand on the seawall and let the wind rock me. But I couldn't go out there.

No one had used the walkway from our back veranda to the river for decades. The concrete was broken and ragged with weeds. The fountain in the center of the walk had been dry for forty years. Even the green slime that had covered the old fishpond had long ago dried up, leaving only a black stain.

But hidden there in raveling vines, the old vines thick and wooden and the young green ones interlocking tight as linen around her, was my goddess, my Lorelei. A celestial being held captive by jungle vines, soft as sculpted moonlight, her dreaming face aglow under deep sea green. As a child, my fingers had lightly traced the liquid curve of her arm, of her breasts, of her pearl-woven rope of hair. I had not been able to see her from my window for years, but I felt her in the heart of me, at my core.

They were predicting that the hurricane would reach land in approximately 48 hours. I checked our supply of candles and matches. Started filling containers with water. My only fear was that the storm would uproot the trees around our house, exposing it.

Gerry was becoming agitated. It wasn't anxiety about the hurricane. I think he was indifferent to the hurricane. Something was after him.

I also feared river rats. If the property were flooded, they could swarm into the house.

In the first decade after Mother died, I started going for long walks along the sea wall. I guess I had a little of Father's adventuresome spirit in me, but not his courage. I always followed the sea wall home. I was tethered to the big white and yellow house on the river.

One evening I did not get back home until dusk. I was hurrying when suddenly a big river rat scurried over the sea wall ahead of me. I rushed to the house, imagining rats everywhere out there in the dark, in the empty fountain, crawling sleek and black and fat over the milk-white shoulder of Lorelei. They were swarming around my feet as I ran nearly crazed into the house. My brother was in the kitchen leaning over the sink, sobbing. His tears falling into the sink. When I rushed in he turned, startled, his face desperate with fear. I knew without any doubt that he thought I had left him. He was so like our mother in that instant, so like the way I had seen her many times in the last months of her life, that the hair rose on the back of my neck. It occurred to me that like our mother, he was losing his mind.

I don't know what happened. Why or when my heart turned against my father. Why in the end I detested him. Why I could not grieve for him. I don't know. I know that he began to change after Mother died.

If I think of him the way he was then, in the dreaming time, I see him standing on the top step of the back veranda, leaning a little, one shoulder against the porch column, drink in hand. He is wearing a white linen suit and he is gazing out over the river, a slight smile on his face. My brother and I were trailing our fingers through the water drops sparkling from the fountain when Father simply appeared there on the veranda above us, his face and linen suit aglow in the last, golden light of day. Like an angel, materializing suddenly and briefly among us.

In hindsight, of course, I realize that he existed that golden afternoon in a perpetual state of drunken tranquility. But there was a spirit in him that transcended even that. The power that was in him trivialized the deadly amber liquid in his glass. The liquor might have been a prop. A woefully, comically inadequate disguise for a being of purest light.

Human beings, blinded by his radiance, missed the small detail of the drink altogether.

While Mother lived, Father was sublime. But the day that life receded from her eyes, as moment by moment she turned to marble in his arms, the light of heaven went out of his eyes forever.

He was only 36 when she died. Still handsome, of course, for many, many years. But the light had gone out of him. He had descended.

His eyes clouded. Growing old, he winced at bright daylight. He did not want to see or to be seen. He started at any sudden sound. Kept away even from the sound of our voices. We seemed to frighten him. As if we, his children, were evidence of some careless transgression. Guilt-ridden, he avoided our eyes. In the end, he was only an old man, ashamed and afraid.

I close my eyes and look up at him again. The burnished column, the white linen suit. I hear the ice tinkle in his glass as he lifts it to his lips, his eyes musing, smiling upon the river. And dreaming him again, I feel the river rising behind me. Dark, enorming. I have to open my eyes quickly to breathe.

My parents had wonderful parties, in the first decade of the century, when muslin and voile still floated on the ladies' arms, about their ankles. On fresh winter evenings they threw open the dining room to the dancing porch that swept out from it in a broad curve to the front of the house and placed tables end to end so that Father, seated at the head of the table in the dining room, was within shouting distance only of Mother at the foot of the table out on the dancing porch. Jacaranda, Sea Grape, Strangler Fig and Royal Poinciana nodded at her back in the soft evening breezes and the flames of the candles down the length of the table whipped, striking lights in faceted crystal wine glasses and decanters, making little dancing shadows on the glowing cheeks of their friends. The deep voices of the young men in the dining room shouted to those out on the veranda. One night, roaring with laughter, they flung ice at one another. The ice hit the polished floor in the dining room and slid against the walls. Chunks of ice shot through the foliage of the trees outside. Mother was out of range, under the table on her hands and knees, sagging with laughter.

I loved my parents' parties.

Mother's lawn parties were fabled. She had them out back of the house, in the gazebo that, with its Doric columns, stood like a small Greek temple on the riverbank. The grounds around the house then were open, the young trees and neat, flowering bushes carefully tended, the grass cut by colored men with lifted shoulders pushing against hand mowers. Above them, as she waltzed barefooted and humming across her bedroom in the latest couture from Paris or New York, Mother occasionally peeped from her windows at her rather large staff of Negro servants moving about on the lawn below, setting her dining table with white damask, creamy, gold-rimmed china, a heavy silver tea service, cut crystal bowls heaped with big, pearl-pink and white roses. I was wandering among these preparations one day when she leaned out her window above us and called to the young woman who was walking across the lawn with silver candelabra in either hand. Mother's voice floated down to us like music. *"Gather gardenias. Float them in the finger bowls."*

At sunset, as the guests began to arrive with the muffled slamming of car doors and laughter, the servants would bring out the champagne buckets, cold and sweating, filled with hand-chipped ice, and arrange beside them sparkling decanters of gin and whiskey and precious little silver bowls of fresh mint leaves, sliced lemon and lime.

Gerry and I would sit on the floor in Mother's bedroom with our chins on the windowsill and watch the beautiful young people parading across the lawn toward the river and the candle-lit gazebo, shimmering in the roseate glow of the setting sun, its slender columns wound with chiffon and garlands of huge, thorny roses.

On one occasion, Mother had the chiffon canopy over the table heaped with rose petals of every hue in our garden and as her guests lifted their glasses in a champagne toast, she had the ties pulled that released the petals. I can hear the music of their laughter as her friends' startled faces lifted to the turning pink and white and pale coral petals that touched their cheeks like velvet kisses and dropped softly into their slender flutes of champagne.

I could not know it at the time, but our wealth was fabulous.

Mother also had boozy, afternoon tea parties for the ladies. These parties went on long after the interlacing slats of the trellis above their heads made crisscross patterns of sun and shadow on the white tablecloth, the golden afternoon fading to lilac twilight when the men arrived, slamming bottles of Cuban rum on the table, laughing, gobbling at their young wives' throats, the women strangling with laughter.

In my dreams Mother's dinner table is afloat upon the dark running river, chiffon rippling in the river breeze, liquid pearls dropping from silver candelabra onto shimmering damask. The young, beautiful faces of the diners are pearled by the candlelight. It is the heavenly vision of a happy child.

Mother had trained the Negro men on her staff to wait upon her guests. She dressed them in white uniforms and gloves. Earnest and bewildered, they played their parts as best they could but finally, observing them slyly, her eyes twinkling with amusement, she would touch Daddy on the arm and he would get up, hand each man a bottle, sit back down and resume his conversation. Furtively, remaining at attention, the waiters drank until they were too drunk to stand. I have seen them slump quietly down on the grass and the guests step over their prostrate bodies. And Father laughing, turning abruptly in search of Mother's lovely face. He loved her, loved her. God in heaven.

Naked, both of them wrapped in chiffon and broken flowers, they danced out there in the starlight after their guests had gone home. I know. I saw them.

I think the girl at the window is waiting for her father.

Mother was strangely beautiful. I mean she had a strange beauty. Her face was changeable. In a certain light and with a certain expression, her face was a poet's vision of beauty. Almost ethereal, her skin like alabaster candle-lit from within, the light shining softly, with heavenly purity from her eyes.

At other times she could be plain almost to homeliness. I don't know what made the difference.

She was always good to us. She was a good mother. Gerry she adored. She couldn't help it. I guess she thought of him as a miniature of his father. She would swing him round and round, cooing nonsense, just as she sometimes played with Father, growling in his ear, nibbling at his ear lobe. But Gerry wasn't much interested in her. His eyes, from the day he was born, yearned for his father.

Father loved us, too, of course. I remember Gerry, when he was little, receiving the affectionate head rubbing and cuffing about that fathers give their sons, and I remember father taking my wrists in his big hands and planting warm kisses in the palms of my little hands.

Thinking back, I realized that Father had been an enormously good-natured person, and for all his intelligence, as essentially light-hearted as I was. I never remember him, in my childhood, being anything but cheerful in the house. He knew how not to suffer. He drank very good bourbon over ice with lime. His finger often poking absently among the ice cubes for the wedge of lime. Sometimes he put the green lime wedge between his teeth and smiled a green-lime-monster smile at us. He was always happy. He was always tender-hearted and merry with us. He was our delight.

But there was something missing. We never got from him what we wanted. He didn't need us. That was it. We wanted to matter as much to him as he did to us. But he seemed to live beyond any need to be loved.

Mother, though, was the very breath of his life. She had what we wanted— his unfailing attention. The full, absolute concentration of his being was upon her and she threw it all away. Just carelessly flung it off her fingertips as I had seen her toss a strand of pearls out her upstairs bedroom window one day.

There were two of my mother. The flesh and blood one, gay, loving, every bit as intelligent as Father and with indefatigable energy, and another, insubstantial one standing always within her with arms outstretched, desperate, imploring. Not all father's love could fill my mother's beautiful arms. Healthy, happy children could not fill them. I think Father tried. But always in her eyes, the ghost stretched out its empty arms.

I think that my mother was afraid. And that Father's only reason for being was to stand between her and whatever awaited her within the darkness of her own imagining. She was a lovely, fairy-like creature under glass, captivated by this being of light who was her husband and her guardian angel, but flitting wildly about, snapping the glass with frantic wings.

Gerry and I, too, stood transfixed in Father's light, especially on that golden afternoon of my eighth birthday.

I do not remember much about that day except that Father gave me a dainty necklace of pearls. Mother had dressed me in my new party frock with a wide, satin sash and I was standing beside her at her dressing table when he came into the room and lowered the pearls over my head, tenderly fastening them in back. I remember the clasp pulled the little hairs on the nape of my neck, giving me a shiver. Mother's gift was to come later, a surprise. He always gave her a gift on my birthday and Gerry's. His gift to her for her gifts to him.

After that, I remember only a moment, the moment that Gerry and I stood by the fountain and looked up at Father standing on the back veranda high above us, leaning against a porch pillar in a white linen suit in the golden glow of early evening. The fountain plashed softly as we yearned up at him, wanting him to look down, to see us.

Then something else happened.

My attention was diverted, I have never known by what, to the party room behind Father. The French doors of the room were open to the veranda and I could almost make out my birthday party in full motion in there with Mother moving like a shadow, dancing through the swirls of smoke, in the green glow of a glass lamp, a cocktail glass uplifted in her hand. In memory, the gramophone disc whirls silently, the lips of the guests move silently. I glimpse only the quick shadow of Mother and then the silence is broken with a shriek and the sound of glass breaking. I look up anxiously into Father's face. He smiles and lifts his glass to his lips.

For the first time in my young life, a shadow fell across my heart.

Is it not possible that angels are dangerous?

The day that Mother died, when he walked toward me, pushing the door shut between us, the shadow moved once again across my heart.

Mother was restless. Before she turned thirty, she stopped having parties. She read and drank a lot. Mother was always coldly furious when she was drinking, in the later years, when she was drinking alone. At such times her fine mind was sharp, unforgiving, precise as an ice pick. Her heart was cold, her vision clear. We kept away from her when she was like this. Our young faces grew troubled.

Mother became gaunt, bitter. Then it was Father who extended empty arms, not imploring her, but offering his compassion. But she shut him out. She wanted to sleep all the time. She needed at least nine, ten hours to feel well, though in the last years no amount of sleep gave her rest. She awoke angry. Sleeping unmoving on her back, each morning she opened bitter eyes to the ceiling. I always remember her being angry with father in the mornings. I could hear their voices, his placating, filled with good humor, with tenderness, and hers furious. I was embarrassed for him. I wondered why he didn't just leave her alone. Because after he was gone, she would calm down, even, at times, approach cheerfulness. It seemed to me that he was deliberately provoking her anger. When she got the cancer, I thought that he had put it in her, as I believed he had put anger and pain in her. It was his fault, everything that was happening. For no other reason than that he let it happen.

When our mother died at the age of 35, she was frightening.

Sayre had been a dreamy young girl. I remember her when I was probably three and Gerry was a baby, the three of us lying back on pillows with gauzy stuff, mosquito netting, draped around us. I think we were in a high place, outdoors, so we must have been on the porch that opened off her bedroom. She lies there, a confection of ribbons and delicate laces, smiling dreamily as her babies play with her hair. Her flesh is creamy as rose petals, her cheeks, lips and fingertips, her toes, the nipples of her small breasts a blush of pink.

I think Mother drew her children with her into her dream state. We became a chimera of her imagination, and she of ours. Our eyes were blinded with a soft, scintillate light.

When she died, it was from her inability to pretend anymore.

I have never liked fairy tales very much. There is always some horror associated with them. Death, in one form or another.

I waited at the foot of the stairs, gripping the newel post so hard my fingertips were numb, until my mother's bedroom door opened and Father came out. As he came down the steps, I glared up at him, hating him. For shutting us out. For keeping her to himself. It was his fault she was dead.

But anymore I don't know. One day I was a girl waiting at the foot of the stairs as Father came down from Mother's room. Then I was this heavy, middle-aged woman waiting at the foot of the steps as Gerry came down from the playroom on the third floor. Why the old man had gone up there to do it we shall never know. I really don't know what happened in either room.

"I think we're in for it, don't you?"

They had finally upgraded Estelle to the status of hurricane. She was sixty miles out to sea, heading straight for us. She had already taken a swipe of people and houses off the coast of Cuba, a swipe twenty miles long and 5 miles wide.

Gerry shrugged. "Looks like it," he said.

"We ought to get under something when it hits. In case it blows the whole top of the house off."

"Maybe I'll go down to the Bradford Hotel and sit it out in the lounge."

"Gerry..."

"Nothing could knock that place down."

"Gerry...."

"Remember how Dad used to come back from there smelling like whiskey and cigars?" It was the first time he had mentioned Father since his death, and absolutely the first time I had heard Gerry call our father "Dad." I was afraid to say anything, to break the spell. For a moment, Gerry seemed happy. I think he was happy about the storm.

"I'd forgotten about that," I said. "Funny that Mother never minded. She'd laugh and grab him in a big bear hug, growling. Remember? I had forgotten all about that." Gerry's eyes clouded and he took a bite of his sandwich. We were in the back parlor, he in his favorite big armchair and me on the edge of my sofa, having our lunch of baloney sandwiches, mine slopped with mustard, his with Miracle Whip salad dressing spread fastidiously, precisely to the edges of the crust.

I had not planned to bring Mother and Father up to Gerry today or any other day. I had been wanting to for some time, but I had not planned to do it today, on the eve of a hurricane.

Trying to sustain the mood, I smiled and said, "I saw Mother one time take a puff of Father's cigar. It was during one of their parties. Everybody laughed. She was always doing something outrageous, you know?"

"Do we have any more Jell-O?"

"No, you finished it last night. If you want something else, I have a piece of that cherry pie left."

"Naw."

"Gerry. I need to ask you something."

Gerry lifted his glass of ice tea and drained it. I watched the sugar that had settled in the bottom of the glass slide into the ice cubes. "I want to ask you about Mother. I know you don't like to talk about her or Father, but I've been thinking about them both a lot and there are a lot of things I don't understand."

"Then you should have asked *them*. I can't tell you anything you don't already know." He got up with his paper plate and his glass in his hands.

"Gerry, don't walk off now. I need to talk to you."

"There's nothing to know," he said and walked off to the kitchen. My blood boiled.

"I'd like to know why my father *killed himself,*" I shot after him. "*Wouldn't you?*" I shouted. No response from the kitchen. I got up and went after him. He was rinsing his glass out at the sink.

"*Wouldn't you?*" I insisted furiously.

Gerry turned calmly to face me. "No, actually, I wouldn't. I don't give a crap." He set his glass down firmly in the sink and started past me.

"You can't mean that."

It surprised me that he stopped. That he had more to say.

"Some things are just better left alone, Clar. Just...just don't..... "

"I don't understand anything that's happened, Gerry. I don't know how I came to be here, how I got to be *me*. I don't know who *you* are anymore. I don't understand why Father left us. I don't even know how I feel about Mother and Father anymore. I'm starting to hate them, and if I do, I'll really lose them. I want them back. I want them back like they were. Gerry, what happened?"

Gerry was staring at the floor, angrily flexing the muscles in his jaws. "No you don't."

"Don't *what*?" I cried.

"Want them back." He half turned from me, putting the flat of his hand against the doorframe and leaning his head on his arm. "There's nothing to understand, Clara. Mother," he said, his voice catching, "died of a cancer. It ate her up alive. She died. That's all." He lifted his head and turned to face me. "Father…"

A look of horror passed through his eyes and he left the room quickly. I stood there alone, listening to the wind buffeting the house.

Finally, I had to shut all the windows. The wind was so strong it was blowing books open and it blew a small lamp off one of the tables in my bedroom.

All night the wind bammed against the windows. Lying in my bed in the dark, I heard a palm frond tear loose and slam against the side of the house downstairs. I wondered if Gerry were asleep or lying awake as I was. I wondered what he might be thinking as he lay in the darkness with a hurricane battering the house. Maybe he was just worrying about the storm, worrying that a tree limb might come through one of the windows or the French doors. I knew that he would not like to see the house damaged. The house had always meant more to him than it did to me. He really would not know where to go if he lost it. I also know that he dreaded the thought of having to hire workmen to come in and repair any damage. He would hate that. Except for the police and undertaker and his helpers who came when Father died, no one but the three of us had been in this house since Mother died forty years ago.

I slept a little. Was awakened by another loud thump on the house. Probably a coconut. Couldn't go back to sleep. Finally I decided to get up and go down to the kitchen and make a cup of tea. I went quietly down the stairs, hoping Gerry wouldn't hear the wood creaking, although with the wind whistling and trees lashing outside, I doubted he could hear anything else.

I was relieved to discover when I flipped the light switch by the kitchen door that we still had electricity. I made my tea and wandered into the parlor, turning on the small lamp beside my sofa. Then I huddled there with the cup of warm tea between my hands, listening to the wind and the tree limbs and fruit fwamming and knocking against the house. It would be a miracle if none of the windows were broken. In unconscious defense of flying glass, my shoulders were drawn in and my knees pressed tightly together, my toes flexed so only the balls of my feet were touching the floor. The entire house was pitch dark except for the little pool of light I was sitting in.

My eyes roamed over the books rising to the ceiling across the room, just outside the glow of my lamp, and in the empty room I heard their voices. The party voices. I saw the green glass lamp glowing far away, dimly. Mother's shadow moved across the lamp.

Setting my cup down, I dropped my face in my hands, rubbing my fingers up and down on my forehead.

And then I grew still. And began to recede, my consciousness withdrawing, as the sea draws powerfully back, gathering into itself, swelling, becoming the agony that was in her, in *Mother, dancing that long ago afternoon through green lamp light, submerged in her own deep sea of loneliness, ghosted...and Father looming, shimmering in white linen,*

smiling, transcendent perfect beyond anything we could imagine
our eyes blinded by the light...

The sea avalanched, plunged to shore, and I was back.

The lamplight on the table beside me flickered, distracting me. We're going to lose the electricity, I thought. I had lost my train of thought. I tried to get back to the afternoon of my eighth birthday party. But I had lost it. Think about the rooms in other houses, I thought. Try to get back into the rooms. The girl at the window, waiting; the skeletal woman on the bed in that decaying house, waiting to die, staring out the window at the moss swinging a little from the limbs of rain-soaked trees.

Thunder rumbled suddenly, like a barrel rolling across the roof. Lightening flashed at the French doors.

The dying woman is grieving for something lost. That's all I could get. Her sense of awful, irrevocable loss.

I sat in my small pool of lamplight, staring, until the light flickered out. The refrigerator stopped. Funny, you never notice the sound of a refrigerator motor until it stops. A shutter suddenly tore loose and began slamming against the front of the house. Tree limbs and fruit thumped the roof. Carefully, I felt for the edge of the table in front of me and stood. I could not see my hand in front of my face. I thought—I'll feel my way back upstairs and slide back into bed. If the storm blows the house away, it blows the house away. Might as well be in my bed.

Climbing the stairs, I felt suddenly and unaccountably, very old. I felt as if my bones had turned to stone. I literally could not move. And then something in my chest broke. The image came to my mind of a piano wire cut, whipping loose, and I floated free. Now I was going very fast and far, wheeling like a Ferris wheel of lights wheeling like children turning cartwheels against the sun across a shattering of sunlight on water and the high thin cries of seagulls and children crying *so bright so bright...*

Sometime just before daylight, the refrigerator started up in the kitchen. The lamp on the table beside the sofa flickered on. The radio in the kitchen sprang to life. A newscaster was reporting on the damage from the hurricane, on the relief efforts underway. By imperceptible degrees, morning light spread across the dusty floor. Beyond the mud-splattered French doors, torn trees dripped wearily over the only visible bit of pewter river water.

The day passed. Faintly from the kitchen drifted the rippling notes of a xylophone and voices singing a commercial for laundry detergent. Later, a comedy program with canned laughter. The news, with updated reports on the damage from Hurricane Estelle, came on at noon, at 6:00, at 10:00. At midnight, the station went off the air.

In the Cuvier house, Sayre hovered at the top of the stairs. "Gerald?"

At 6:00 a.m. the radio in the kitchen started up with the National Anthem. At 10:00 that morning a truck from the electric company crept up the muddy street in front of the house and parked. Two men got out, moving about cautiously, wary of snakes and downed power lines.

On the third night following the hurricane, the headlights of a police car suddenly filled the parlor window. A few moments later, the flashlights of policemen played over the walls of the room. People were walking around the house, talking. The beams of the flashlights motioned over broken tree limbs, across a window shutter lying on the ground, across ruined fruit. Suddenly, knuckles rapped the kitchen door.

Then pounding. A fist pounding a door. A voice outside, calling. "Mizz Cuvee-airrr? Mizz Cuvee-airr?" Fists pounding. A shaft of light shot across the kitchen floor and big men in uniform came in, crowding in, moving from the kitchen into the parlor, moving around the parlor and finally to the stairs.

"This place gives me the goddamn heebie-jeebies," one of the cops said.

"Jesus Christ."

"*Jesus* H...." The men stood with their hands over their noses and mouths, staring at the body slumped halfway up the staircase.

"Christ, what a stink. Come on. Let's get out and call the coroner. I can't stand this."

"God*damn*. How old *was* this old broad?"

THE SHADOW OF A DREAM

Fifty years later, on a Sunday morning in April, Mrs. Dulcet slid her key into the lock on the side door of the Cuvier House and stepped into the gift shop, a room that in the original house had been the kitchen. Hearing the floor boards creak above her head, Mrs. Dulcet raised her eyes to the ceiling, smiling. Ghosts disturbed her not in the least. She was so fond of the ghostly Cuviers in fact, that she was glad to have at least one of them still in the house.

Mrs. Dulcet knew more than anyone alive about the mysterious Cuvier family. She had researched the family back through Florida and Louisiana to its roots in France in the 18th century, finding quite an abundance of ancestral information but precious little about the Cuviers who had occupied this house. But the mystery was part of the allure of the house.

Mrs. Dulcet was in her third decade as a high school history teacher when the old Cuvier house was purchased by the National Historic Trust. She had eagerly answered the ad for a curator and won the position by the sheer force of her enthusiasm. As one anxious to preserve whatever vestiges of its history remained to her native town, she had lamented for years the deplorable neglect of the Cuvier house. For years after the death of the last of the Cuvier family in 1959, the house had been abandoned. No one claimed it. The city would not buy the property. In the sixties, real estate speculators were buying up huge tracts outside town for housing subdivisions and then shopping centers. The heart of Las Palmas began to decay. Offices closed. Merchants leased space in the new shopping centers out on land that months before had been nothing but sand, palmettos and scrawny pine woods. The once fine homes in town lost their value, decayed and withered like old people. Some of the old homes were bulldozed, others turned into boarding houses for vagrants.

Lawns became weedy yards, littered with trash. Though a chain link fence had been put up around the old Cuvier place to keep out vagrants and vandals, teenagers often sneaked onto the property to smoke and drink and have sex. All the furniture had been stripped from the house, and every window smashed. The house and grounds were overrun with rats. In the late eighties, by the time the house was claimed as a National Historic Landmark, the floors were unstable and graffiti covered the walls. Of course, there had been rumors of ghosts since the corpse of the old Cuvier woman was found in the house after the hurricane of '59.

Mrs. Dulcet's monologue, as she conducted tours of the house, included a reference to the rumor of ghosts. Tourists expected to hear about ghosts. They hoped for ectoplasmic evidence of ghosts in their photographs. Mrs. Dulcet was happy, with twinkling eyes, to tell them the stories of paranormal experiences other visitors had had, but unless in private conversation with a seriously interested visitor, she would not talk about her own, or share her conviction that the house was, as they say, haunted. Each evening as she was closing up she would linger a moment, listening. She had heard voices. They could call her a batty old woman all they wanted to, but she had heard voices, *after* turning off the television in her office. And upstairs, in the room above the former kitchen, she often heard that creaking sound, as if someone were shifting his or her weight from foot to foot. It was a steady, rhythmic sound, very like a rocking chair on a wood floor. Mrs. Dulcet had always hoped to see one of them, but so far, neither Sayre nor Gerald nor either of their children had manifested.

Visitors to the home were few. Most tourists, like the natives, preferred to spend their leisure time at the beach or out in the Gulf fishing, sailing, jet-skiing. On this particular April Sunday, for instance, Mrs. Dulcet had only one visitor. A middle-aged woman came in who seemed enthralled with the house. She gazed about her in wonder. When greeted by Mrs. Dulcet, she immediately explained her eagerness to tour the house.

"I've wanted to get in here all my life," Jessica said breathlessly.

In the early fifties, when Jessica was a small child, she had lived just down the street in a house built about the same time as the Cuvier house, though her house was not nearly so grand, she said. As a child, walking by the Cuvier property, she had been fascinated by what seemed to her the story-book quality of the house. In its lush, tropical setting, she could see little of it but the widow's walk, in her memory white and precious as the ornament on a wedding cake against a brilliant blue sky. She had been told that an old woman still lived in the house but she never saw any evidence of anyone alive in the house at all. Sometimes she crossed the street from her house to the river and walked along the seawall to the Cuvier property. She would ease on to the property, afraid of being seen, and sneak to the "mermaid" by the fish pond. Jessica was captivated by the statue. The curves of her body were liquid, graceful as cool, slow-curling milk. Her small, perfect face was tilted downward on a neck as gently curved as the stem of a new flower. The thick braid trailing over one soft shoulder was intertwined with a rope of pearls and her dainty white fingertips, pearl-like themselves, hovered just above the teeth of the comb beside her on the bench. Jessica would run her fingers lightly over the globes of the pearls, along the folds of her "mermaid's" flowing garment, and the teeth of her comb, touching with reverence the cold, delicate fingertips upon the comb.

"That was Lorelei," Mrs. Dulcet explained, "not a mermaid. Lorelei was the siren in German legend who lured sailors onto the rocks with her singing. There is a song about her but I couldn't quote it now for the life of me."

"Is she still there?"

"Goodness no. She was moved to the lawn in front of the library, where she was, I might add," Mrs. Dulcet said angrily, "decapitated. They never found her head."

"God no. Don't tell me that."

Mrs. Dulcet nodded, her lips tight. Then she quickly went on. "After our tour today, before you leave, you'll want to see the souvenir statues of Lorelei in our gift shop. We have alabaster paper weights and less expensive little resin figures."

"Oh, I'd love one," Jessica cried.

Mrs. Dulcet smiled. "I thought you might. You know, the original Lorelei was quite famous in Las Palmas when the Cuviers lived in this house. Mr. Cuvier had her shipped from Italy not long after he and Mrs. Cuvier arrived. Apparently as a wedding gift. An extravagant gift, to say the least. The newspaper here printed a picture of Lorelei on the front page. It is reputed to be an exact likeness of Sayre."

"Sayre?"

"Mrs. Cuvier."

Jessica turned, bending to read the description of a photo in the gallery of photos on the foyer wall to her left. She read aloud:

"The children of Sayre Alice Randolph Cuvier and Gerald Chamblis Cuvier, Clara Ann and Gerald Chamblis Cuvier VI, age eight and five respectively. September 8, 1909." The children

were beautifully and expensively dressed. Even in the faded old photograph, Jessica could see that.

"These people must have been wealthy," she said.

"Oh my yes. I'm afraid their wealth was legendary. The picture you're looking at was taken on the occasion of Clara Ann's eighth birthday party. It's a shame so little is known about the child…"

"I think I saw her."

Mrs. Dulcet looked blankly at her visitor.

"I mean way back, when I was a little girl. I could swear one day when I was standing out on the sidewalk there I saw a woman's face at a window…." Jessica looked up and pointed at the ceiling "…up there, on the second floor. Naturally I don't remember what she looked like it was so long ago. I just have the faintest memory of a face, like a blur, at the window."

Jessica looked back with a smile at the little girl in the photograph with ribboned hair and a wide satin sash. The children were standing in front of a fountain garlanded with flowers. The boy was in knee-britches, one plump, bare knee resting on the edge of the stone fountain. Both the children were frowning, probably at the sun in their eyes.

"To think that I actually saw this little girl when she was an old woman." Jessica glanced at her guide. Mrs. Dulcet was shaking her head with a sad smile.

"No, no, my dear. You never saw this girl."

"Well, somebody…"

"You must not know the story then…."

"What story? I know nothing whatever about these people."

Mrs. Dulcet hesitated, searching for the appropriate words. "The children were both...lost. Very young. What makes this particular photograph so poignant, in fact, is that it was taken just hours before they died."

Jessica straightened, frowning.

"Yes, well, you see, it was, as I say, little Clara Ann's birthday. Her father had had one of those new electric iceboxes shipped down from somewhere up north. As far as I know, it was the first in the whole state at that time. The story goes that he ordered it for the sole purpose of preserving the birthday party ice cream his servants were making days ahead of the party. They were making, if you can believe it, mint julep ice cream."

At Jessica's amused expression, Mrs. Dulcet smiled and nodded. "Oh yes, the Cuvier parties were beyond imagining, my dear. At any rate, sometime late in the day, after the ice cream had been taken out of the icebox, the children climbed in."

Jessica's lips parted.

"You can imagine how hot it was in early September. And in those days, of course, there was no air conditioning. They probably got in to cool off. For fun." Mrs. Dulcet paused. "They shut the door."

"Dear God."

"No one knows how long they were in there before they were found. There was a party in progress. Who would have thought to keep track of the children? In those days, you know, children just went and played. Parents called them in at supper time, and then again at bed time. But I guess eventually they were missed and the search began. Later, the father is quoted in the newspaper about...what happened. He said that when he finally thought of the icebox, he knew they were in it. People who had been at the party, who had witnessed the tragedy, were also interviewed. One said that when Mr. Cuvier put his hand on the handle of the icebox to open the door, he almost passed out."

Tears stood in Mrs. Dulcet's eyes. "And here's the saddest part. Mr. Cuvier mentioned particularly that when he opened that horrible, beaten door, all Clara Ann's little pearls came dropping out. He had given her a little pearl necklace for her birthday and in her agony she must have torn them off."

Jessica stared at Mrs. Dulcet, her jaw slack.

"They think the boy died first, being the younger of the two, and that little Clara Ann probably died a few minutes later. The oxygen just gave out. And she must have been using it up very fast the way she was kicking at that door to get out."

"And no one heard...?"

"Apparently not."

"What happened to those poor parents?" Jessica leaned toward the picture of Gerald and Sayre on their wedding day in October of 1900.

"They lived in near total seclusion after that. He lived until 1952. She died seven or eight years later. It was before, or during, or after that big hurricane Estelle we had that year. After the storm the police stopped in to see if she was all right. She was so old, you know. They had to go over the property, looking for downed power lines, so they knocked on the doors, and when she failed to come to the door, they forced one of them. Found her on the staircase to the second floor. She had been deceased for several days."

"Wait wait wait a minute. Then if I saw somebody at the window looking back at me when I was a kid, it was..."

"Sayre. You saw Sayre, my dear."

The tremendous commotion of the storm, the pressure against the house, the pushing against the walls has stopped. Sayre is free, as if the line that tethered her to sound and substance had been cut. She drifts up the hollow staircase. Confused, her vision dimming, she peers around her at walls and windows and doors that seem to hover, detached from any physical reality, in a deepening gloom.

Distantly, from the direction of the kitchen below her, she hears a radio coming to life. She passes beyond range of the sound and Gerald is walking down the steps from the third floor landing, coming down in his bathrobe, an old man. She is perplexed. When did Gerald grow old? But she is glad to see him. *Gerald...I thought you were dead.* He passes through her and vanishes. Sayre hears a muted siren but the sound passes away as she moves up the staircase and down along the hallway toward her bedroom thinking *where are the children?* She peers about her, trying to distinguish form in the darkness and fear suddenly closes like a hand around her throat. The children are near, hiding. Sayre peers into the blackness of an abyss. She knows they are near, huddled in the deepest gloom, cowering. Terrified now that she will feel the brush of a garment against her bare leg, the touch of a child's fingertip, she leaves the room instantly.

Hovering at top of stairs, Sayre hears voices below stairs. They are a soft humming. She does not know who the people in the house are. She moves through the rooms upstairs. They are different somehow and obscured by a gloom she can't penetrate. Where is Gerald? He was with her in this house for a long time. She is certain that he was here. She remembers him moving quietly about. Bringing her small dishes of food, glasses of water. Bending over her, running a trembling hand over the top of her head, barely touching her hair. He went in and out the door.

Gerald?

Sayre is moving quickly now, pursued by a low, monotonous jabbering of voices. *Gerald why did you bring me here to save you to save to you to save you nothing can save me save me I wanted to know but why? your brother Gerry is sailing away to China today he's down by the river ready to set sail but Father will not shhhhhhhhhhh don't talk about it Gerald not now not ever why did they mix in two spoonfuls instead of one Gerry come here if I was the queen and you were the king I would cut off your head why won't you let me see her why Father why Father why Father I love you Gerald Chamblis Cuvier but in the end she was too sick and Richard Cory one calm summer night she she she she was crackers crackers hahahahaha and you are crackers too too too and Sayre closed her eyes and let her head fall back, smiling, as little Gerry stroked her face and throat with a long, fluffy feather.*

Where are the children. They are hiding from her. Sayre moves in and out of the rooms, up and down the third and second floor hallways. She knows that they are huddled in a corner of one of the rooms, terrified, but the gloom grows denser. She will never be able to find her children in this shadow land where the furniture, the walls are insubstantial. She reaches into the darkness but can touch nothing. Her heart is breaking.

Gerald is sitting in his chair in the library downstairs. He is freshly bathed and shaved, his hair still wet from his bath and slicked straight back, parting naturally in the middle. His shirt is fresh, crisp, open at the throat. He is perfect, opalescent, like a fashion picture in a magazine. He gazes fixedly at her; without expression.

Sayre stares at him. "Where are the children?" Her voice is loud, real. Gerald's eyes shift, as if he sees something beside or behind her and Sayre turns her head, searching the darkness with frightened eyes. When she turns back to Gerald, he is gone.

Why has her left her, suddenly? He was her home. Coming quickly, as soon as he heard, mounting the stairs two at a time. Her mother was gone and she was lost, floating, falling and he came up the stairs on a few long strides furiously without concern without thought of Father below, throwing open her bedroom door against every law of propriety and decency he strode in and folded her in his arms and Father standing at the foot of the stairs, looking up, afraid of him now, not daring to come up, to protest. They heard the door of his study slam.

They are sailing swiftly, swift as flight, airborne, up the broad and shining river, she, Sayre, and her beautiful husband and the house is coming and the house is coming, white and pale, creamy yellow, pretty as a wedding cake.

Clara shoves aside the magazines and books on the broad coffee table and sets down two small salad plates, each with a cheese and tomato sandwich sweetened with Miracle Whip salad dressing that she had slopped on with jerking hands, fiercely shaking the salt and pepper shakers over them. Gerry likes his tomatoes heavily salted and peppered. When Clara sits down, she is facing not her brother Gerry, but Gerald.

Gerald is looking at his fingers, pulling strongly on each in turn. He looks older than Clara remembers him. Worn. Lines around his eyes. The golden glow that had seemed to emanate from him since his boyhood is gone.

When Gerald finally glances up at her, his face is ruined with shame. "I'm sorry," he says. His voice comes not from him but from someplace deep within or beyond him.

He vanishes from the chair.

"Gerald?"

Sayre hears a trickling sound. She senses that the walls around her, in the darkness, are fluid. Now she is kneeling by a bed on the bare floor of a bare-walled room. A bureau stands against the wall by the window. The sky outside is sodden with just spent rain. A breeze, cold after the rain, stirs the Spanish moss hanging from the limbs of the old oak outside the window. The rain had come down like a wall of water as she knelt by the bed, gazing across the bed and out the open window opposite. Sayre had gazed out the window while the rain blew in upon the floor, misting her young, pallid face, misting the grey lips of the corpse on the bed. Sayre had watched the rain blow into the room, her arms all goose bumps, and would not turn her eyes down to the empty thing on the bed that had been her mother.

Sayre is standing in her bathroom upstairs, trying to understand where she is. She remembers lying in the bathtub, the room thick with steam, the water warm over her breasts, the light overhead making rainbows in the steam. The rainbows swirl, making her dizzy. Gerry, in shorts and white shoes, is shaking one of her bottles of cologne. The cologne bubbles in the swirled pink and lavender glass. Gerry is frowning with the intensity of his effort to keep the cologne water bubbling and sparkling. Sayre laughs and reaches to cup her hand under the bottle.

Glass is showering across the floor, rising light as mist around her reaching hands, the heavy, beaded sleeve of her deep sea green dress.

Sayre sits on the edge of the sofa, angry, embarrassed. "Mother was sick, *sick.*"

"No," Gerald says quietly. "She was insane. Sayre..."

"She was sick, Gerald."

"Sayre, your mother was insane. You didn't know that?"

Sayre speaks slowly, carefully. "I know she was changed...in the end...but that's because she was sick..."

"She was slowly going insane. All those years. Your father knew it."

Sayre's face heated. She stood. "Gerald, I'm tired of this. And I'm sorry, but I'm tired of you. I wish you'd go away."

Gerald gazes up at her hopelessly. He starts to speak.

"Just stop."

"Sayre, look."

Gerald extends his hand, his dirty boy's fingers lightly closed over his palm. His playmate leans to see and Gerald slowly uncurls his fingers. The firefly pulses once against his palm and flies away. Panting with delight, the boy leans to Sayre for a kiss. His baby breath in her face is warm and smells faintly of sour milk. Sayre is filling with so much love for this boy that she is afraid her heart will explode she has to open her mouth to breathe kissing boys is forbidden Miss Sayre Alice Randolphe even if it is Gerald Mama tell me again about the babies the scent of lilacs lilacs the healthy heavy babies in christening gowns trailing over our arms the sunlit morning so lovely and lilacs in the churchyard lilacs in the rinse water the linen white and crisp in the cool cold dark chancel and the baby boy awakening look

*darling look say hello to Sayre Alice and hurry Mama tell me
again what you saw saw saw*

"I saw it in his eyes. He knew you."

and then what Mama what what

Sayre hears her mother's voice clearly in the empty
room "Gerald's mother was startled; she laughed at the sudden
lift of the baby's head from her arm."

I love that story the best, Mama.

Mrs. Dulcet turned and led Jessica from the foyer of the
house into the parlor to their right. "The rumors began almost
instantly," she continued. "That Sayre was never seen again
because she had gone insane. That her husband was keeping
her locked up in here because she was a dangerous lunatic.
You know how people like to exaggerate. Personally I don't
think she was anything of the kind. Yes, certainly she had been
pushed beyond the limits of endurance or sanity by her grief,
but I doubt she was a raving maniac or that Mr. Cuvier ever
had her locked up. It was just that her life was ended, that's all.
Mr. Cuvier came into town infrequently, for groceries and such.
Was polite if spoken to, but could not be engaged in
conversation."

"How did he die?"

"Heart just gave out. The police received a call one day
from someone who didn't give her name. Just said quietly into
the phone, 'You may come and get my father' and in just as
calm and collected a tone as you please, gave her exact street
address. The police couldn't get here fast enough. Couldn't wait
to get in here and see whatever there was to see. But here's
what happened. When they came up the steps to the front

door, the door was standing ajar. She had left it open for them. But she was nowhere to be seen. The body was laid out in the foyer here where we stand, here on the floor. Well, they had wanted to get into the house, but they could hardly invade the woman's privacy and go farther than the body, so they left. Very letdown I may say. Said as they were going down the steps they heard the front door close softly and the bolt turn. She was never seen after that by a living soul."

"Wait now. Go back. I thought you said it was her husband who died."

"Yes."

"But she told the police to come and get her father."

"Oh yes. That was no slip of the tongue. Those were her exact words. People have wondered about that ever since. Of course there is no one living now who ever knew them, who might be able to shed light on the mystery. The young people they knew back at the turn of the century were probably all gone by the time Mr. Cuvier died. In any case, their friends faded away very quickly after the tragedy. It's said very few even attended the children's funeral. People don't know what to do or say in the face of something like that. One can hardly blame them."

"But I don't understand...if he was her husband, why would she call him her father?"

Mrs. Dulcet sighed. "I have an opinion but..."

"Give."

Mrs. Dulcet laughed. "No, no. I'd rather not get into that. I may have my thoughts, but goodness knows, I wouldn't presume to say."

"Presume to say."

"Well, I..."

"You know something."

"No, I really don't. But I...."

Jessica sighed and looked stern.

"Oh, all right then. I have thought about it, about her last words, the last words anyone ever heard her say. I don't know, but it occurred to me—that—you asked me, so now so I'm going to tell you—I think she did a mind transference or whatever you call it. *I* think that Sayre thought her husband was her *father*. I mean, she knew that the man in the house was Gerald Cuvier. I just think she thought he was her father. That she was *his daughter*."

"I don't quite—I don't get it."

Mrs. Dulcet took a deep breath. "I'm saying that I think...I think *Sayre thought she was Clara Ann.*"

Jessica looked blankly for a moment at Mrs. Dulcet. "Is that possible?"

Mrs. Dulcet shrugged. "Stranger things..." she began. "But you see, it would be a way to get the children back. To *be* them. One of them, at least. And maybe in her mind little Gerry was in there with her. And Gerald, Mr. Cuvier was their father. Naturally, since he was, in fact, the father of the children. At times, perhaps, he was little Gerry grown up. Who knows? Who can ever know what went on in her mind? If she had a mind left after what happened."

A little embarrassed by her confession of this astonishing theory, Mrs. Dulcet cleared her throat and indicating the room in which they stood with a sweep of her arm, began the official tour of the house, explaining that the furnishings were not original to the house, of course, but that, as far as they were able to determine, the original furnishings and layout of the rooms had been replicated. Frowning, only half listening, Jessica followed Mrs. Dulcet into the dining room. Warming to her favorite subject, Mrs. Dulcet described with pleasure the extravagant and somewhat scandalous dinner parties the Cuviers had had in their youth. As she talked, Mrs. Dulcet's eyes occasionally slid to and quickly off Jessica's face. It was apparent that Jessica was not fully engaged in her stories; clearly, she was still grappling with the "mind transference" theory.

With a fixed smile, Mrs. Dulcet led her visitor upstairs to the second-floor bedrooms, explaining that the third floor was used for storage and not admissible to visitors. In the room that Sayre had occupied until her death, Mrs. Dulcet pointed out the picture of Sayre's parents in an ornate (though somewhat tarnished) silver frame on the dresser. "It's a copy, of course. The original was a daguerreotype, a bit cloudy, so the reproduction has been touched up a bit. Obviously, this portrait was made on their wedding day." The woman in the portrait stood beside her husband, who was seated, her right hand resting on his shoulder. In the fashion of the day, they were unsmiling, as befitted the dignity of the occasion.

"It's impossible to tell by this photograph what these people really looked like. They are obviously well-off. Her wedding costume is expensively made. Probably in Paris. At the very least in Boston or New York." Mrs. Dulcet sighed. "But the family is sadly—shall I say—haunted by tragedy."

Jessica lifted her brows in sardonic consent. *"Now what?"*

"When she was still a relatively young woman, Sayre's mother succumbed to some sort of mental illness, and died—from what, precisely, I have not been able to discover. I think the actual cause of her death may never be known. In any event, when Sayre was twenty, her mother died in an abandoned house on the family estate, a house that was subsequently left to her caretakers, two Negro women who had been family servants. Nothing much is known about the father, other than that he was born in 1857 to the famed Randolphe family." Mrs. Dulcet rested her fingertips lightly on the picture frame. "We don't know what became of Sayre's father after her mother's death. Sayre was their only child and within days of her mother's death, she and Gerald Chamblis Cuvier were married and immediately left Louisiana and came away here, making their way in 1900 up the Caloosa River to Las Palmas. Apparently this house was a wedding present. I can only conjecture, but I imagine that Gerald and Sayre were running away from the scandal of her mother's insanity. In those days, of course, insanity was generally believed to be inherited. Sayre might have been running from that presumption. Certainly, where she grew up and was known, people might have been eyeing her strangely, with that expectation. In any case, when the children died and she shut herself up, or was shut up, in this house, people said she had gone insane and died like her mother died. Well, if she did, it was not without cause."

"Ghosts?" Jessica asked, with a smile.

Mrs. Dulcet returned the smile, delighted to have Jessica's full attention once again.

"I think someone is here."

"Which one?"

"One would have thought the children perhaps, given the circumstances of their death. But I don't sense children. Nor is it a man's energy. I think it is Sayre."

Jessica gazed up and around at the walls, the ceiling. "How could she get out? If she died not even knowing who she was, how could she ever find her way out?"

"Precisely."

Sayre drifts swiftly down the staircase. She is becoming fear. As fear she moves through her party guests, through the shadows of people in motion around her, their voices and laughter swirling through her head. Someone is winding the gramophone and the music begins with a low growl as if it were coming from the echo chamber of a cave. In the dark, phantasmal room, points of light flicker from the clothing of people circling in dance motion around her and gradually the room is brightening, color swimming into the clothing, into the faces of the people. They are alive, and she is back.

"Sayre, where have you been? Gerald's been looking all over for you."

She stands looking into the face of the man speaking to her. He is smiling, his eyes fond, curious, concerned. She moves past him or through him, trying to understand how she came to be here. She can't remember these people. She can't remember how they came to be here. She cannot feel her own substance.

Now they are drawing back from her, stepping back to make way for Gerald. He is walking toward her from the back veranda. He has a drink in his hand. He is smiling. She feels the pearls cold against her breast, ice cream dripping down the cleavage of her breasts. She runs the pearls between her lips, cream gathering in a minty lather at the corners of her mouth. She runs her tongue deliciously over her lips, her eyes wicked. Gerald's face moves in close. She tilts back her head to give him her lips.

Fear grips her throat like a hand. Where are the children? Where are my children? Gerald has vanished. The people in the room are restless, sickened. They set down their glasses as if the liquid in them were poisoned. The gramophone growls to a stop.

Hovering at the foot of the stairs, confused, Sayre hears a shattering of glass.

Amid glass falling like crushed ice, like snow, tiny pearls are hopping about Gerald's shoes, his gleaming brown and white, two-tone shoes, the pearls raining from the icebox, tatting the floor around Gerald's feet and a woman is screaming. A woman is screaming in Sayre's head as she bends to help Clara Ann into the icebox, little Gerry's round, freckled face looking up at her from inside his own smaller compartment, the five-year-old grinning up with baby teeth at his mother she is having trouble with Clara the girl's thin arm not wanting to bend, to go inside, the girl's thin white arm pushing back but she has her hands on Clara Ann's shoulders, pushing her down, pushing her into a box so she can keep her daughter small imploring her to understand Father will see the cracks in your head like he saw Mother's and the rain will get inside and rot you like it did Mother and Father will put you in that house she's dead in there she whispered as she stuffed her children into the icebox to preserve and save them from her father was walking toward her where she stood waiting outside her mother's door to get in and he walked to the door and quietly closed it in her face as Sayre pushed back on Clara Ann's thin white arm bringing down quickly the heavy lid of the ice box, the beaded sleeve of her green silk dress dropping over Sayre's wrist as the door shut with the suction seal of a vacuum.

Gerald is walking toward the icebox. She is behind him. The icebox grows larger and larger as they walk toward it Gerald white around the mouth like he is going to vomit as he reaches for the handle on the door knowing that the children who have kept the secret of the Mother's pearls hidden in the ice cream for days would not have missed the moment Mother pulled them from the ice cream for anything on earth but he has not seen them since they were playing at the fountain, since the servants took the ice cream out of the icebox, since he heard shrieks of delight from the room behind him and turned, his guests parting before him and strode toward Sayre standing by a great, cut-glass punch bowl, the pearls that he had pushed into the ice cream now uplifted in her hands, cold pearls dripping sticky cream onto her warm breasts as she brings the pearls to her lips and runs them through her mouth, the creamy lather gathering on her lips, her eyes wicked.

"Where are the children?" someone cried.

Heads turn, the realization that the children are missing going around the room just before their lips touch and he hesitates, wondering, his eyes seeing the flicker of knowing in Sayre's, the movement of the shadow through her eyes as she turns her head toward the kitchen, the icebox growing as he comes nearer and nearer, his knees folding, knowing that his children are not outside playing they are in the icebox.

They have found the children, Sayre thinks, and means to move into them, to move them aside, to find at last the faces of her children but she cannot move into or among them. She pushes as if against an invisible glass, whimpering.

The pearls dropped out first. Then Clara Ann's thin arm flopped out, palm up, small fingers loosely curled. The tips of the fingers white as pearls. One of the servants, seeing the child's arm drop from the icebox, let the empty, cut-glass punch bowl he had brought in from the parlor slip through his fingers. Sayre's fractured mind shattered with it, exploded into the reflective shards through which she would move as wind through glass prisms, the mirrors turning and tinkling, her own lost face, in all its reflections, flowing through them.

The firefly, with slow, ethereal pulsations of light, beats her wings against the glass, gasping for breath, smothering.

Mrs. Dulcet and Jessica descend the stairs, hands trailing along the banister to their right. Jessica is sharing with Mrs. Dulcet her own theory that ghosts are merely the life energy of disincarnate people, nothing so very wu*hooo-ooo* about it but actually only very sad for the so-called "ghosts," who—Sayre hears their voices but their words are indistinguishable as they pass through the place her mind occupies at the foot of the empty staircase in an empty house in the darkness of a dream, of deep memory. In Sayre's house, the headlights of a car, coming off the bridge toward the house, sweep across the window. Sayre moves about the house as the shadow of a sheer curtain moves, lifting and folding and opening across a moonlit floor. Her energy ebbs and flows, like the slow pulsations of a beating heart.

Sayre is impacted suddenly with a force that seems to lunge through her. It divides her. She feels the living energy of her body as she pounds up the staircase screaming, "*Get them out. They can't breathe.*" She rushes into the bedroom as Gerald turns, his face startled. She hurls herself on him, beating her fists against his chest. *"You put my children in **boxes**...in **boxes** under the **ground**...GET THEM OUT. THEY CAN'T BREATHE."*

Sayre feels his fists around her wrists. She is struggling on the bed, her wrists locked under her back. She feels his fingers in her mouth, his knuckles against her teeth, forcing them apart. She is gagging on the pills he pushes down her throat until she swallows convulsively. Locked down, unable to move, she drifts down softly into memory dreaming herself Clara sitting across the low, broad, magazine-strewn coffee table from her brother Gerry.

"Clara. Your mother killed herself."

She is tight-lipped with fury. "But she lost all that weight. She had cancer. Father said she had a cancer and that's why he had to send her away. He said I might catch it."

"You can't catch cancer, Clar."

"I didn't know that then."

"Did you ever see a doctor come to the house?"

"Father said she was sick."

"He was trying to protect you."

Gerald leaned toward Sayre. Her eyes drifted.

"Sayre, listen to me."

She frowned. "Why are you calling me by that name? Why are you saying her name?"

"Sayre, look at me."

She looked at him, frowning her displeasure.

"She poisoned herself. She was slowly poisoning..."

"Shut your mouth."

"...herself and when your father found out about it...

Sayre threw her hands over her ears.

"...he put her away in that old house, nearby, so Mary and Jenny could take care of her but by then it was too late and he told you she was sick so you would never know so nobody would ever know what he could never let anyone, especially you, ever find out...."

"I hate your living guts."

Sayre is sitting at the dressing table in her bedroom, her head turned slightly toward the window to her left. Far below, in the elliptical drive, Joe stings the rump of the horse with a steel-tipped buggy whip. The light phaeton jerks into view, rounding the drive, the sleeve of her mother's nightdress fluttering at the open window. They have taken her mother away in her nightdress in the daytime. Mother is sick. Father has disposed of her.

Sayre stands just inside the front door of the house. Her father stands at the other end of the breezeway that extends the width of the great house from the entrance to the back door. They stand a moment looking at each other, the distance lengthening between them. Then her father turns and steps out the door, vanishing as if he had dropped off a cliff.

Sayre stands where he had stood, looking down at the tracks of his wet shoes on the floor. A sudden breeze blows the smell of rain in her face.

Sayre, in black, barefooted, runs screaming up the stairs. Gerald takes her in his arms, locks her down, and she dreams, the images in her mirroring mind merging and emerging *as she drifts down the hallway to her bedroom drifting through the door and across the room and running her arms through the glass, the jagged pieces of window glass raking channels in her slender white arms. She turns, holding her arms out to her children sheets of blood running down each arm into the palms of her hands and pouring through her fingers onto the floor. In her dream the room is so quiet that she can hear the drops of blood tapping the floor. She is speaking, but her voice is weak and she cannot hear the words that the Sayre in the mirror is saying to her. Gerald enters the room. She is sitting between her two children under the broken window, leaning back against the wall in blood and glass.*

She hears Gerald's voice. "You are dreaming. Sayre, you are dreaming."

"Sayre, this did not happen to you."

But it is happening. Her hand is crawling weakly over her son's small hand on the floor beside her. His hand feels spidery. Cold. She is trying to lift the small hand. She doesn't want Gerald to take him away from her. Her running blood soaks her legs, flows into her children's clothes so warm so warm as weakly she picks at her boy's fingers because Clara Ann is already dead picking at her little boy's fingers as if she were plucking flowers...whispering...there's a daisy...a daisy. She drops her head back against the wall whispering as Gerald walks towards her, I would give you some violets, but they withered all when my father died. He bends and lifts her up. Puts his hands under her arms and lifts her. Lays her gently on the bed. Walks to the door where Clara waits. Shuts the door quietly in her face.

On a day in early February of 1908, Sayre Cuvier stood gazing out the French doors of her beautiful home toward the Caloosa River far across the back lawn. At the fiery end of day, the mile-wide river ran like lava, shimmering with crusted gold.

Sayre glided across the lawn, gazing at the river. She sat in the gazebo and her small son, Gerry, wandered to her. Silently, she drew him to stand between her knees. Gerry let his head fall back against his mother's breast. His small hands rested on her thighs. Mother and son gazed silently at the fiery, flowing river.

After a while, Sayre began to lift and drop each of Gerry's tiny fingers in turn, whispering, *"There is a willow grows aslant a brook."*

As the sun slid below the horizon, a chill crept into the yet golden afternoon and the wind picked up, whipping a tendril of Sayre's hair across her child's face. The warmth of his body against her breast felt good. Her breath was warm in his ear.

"There with fantastic garlands did she come..." Sayre's eyes filled with tears, filling her vision of the river with tears and she was floating farther and farther away, her whispers following. *"Of crow-flowers, nettles, daisies, and long purples...down...down... her clothes spread wide...and, mermaid-like, awhile they bore her up...which time she chanted snatches of old tunes...as one incapable of her own distress...but how long it could not be...till that her garments, heavy with their drink, pulled the poor wretch from her melodious lay...to muddy death."*

Sayre leaned forward to look into her son's face. "Do you understand, my darling?"

His face was featureless, dissolving in her tears as slowly, the waters closed over her head.

Tra la la, twiddle dee dee dee

It gives me a thrill,

To wake up in the morning

To the mockin'bird's trill.

Clara heard the lilting melody of the mockingbird song and smiled and sipped her tea and a cooling breeze smelling gloriously like rain caressed her face and then the picture in the newspaper, the grainy image of the old refrigerator, its beaten door hanging open, moved into her eyes and her brother Gerry said sharply,

"Sayre."

She reached into the darkness, blind, unable to find him.

"Sayre, it's not your fault."

She could not see him. Suddenly, she felt herself wrapped in his arms. She could feel his heart beating strongly against her ear. He guided her to a chair and sat her down. She could see nothing. She felt her hands clenched in her lap only when his hands, big and warm, closed over them.

Gerald knelt before Sayre. Shrunken, grey, trembling, she cowered before him like a woman twice her age, the bones of her shoulders drawn protectively close. He would never know on what day all those years ago, in the bright happy days, in the dreaming time, that her mind turned, like a man turning on his heel and leaving a room, like a man turning and stepping off a cliff. He saw her standing one day with the palms of her hands lifted, her fingers slightly spread. She was staring at her empty hands, her body rocking slightly forward and back and the realization that her mother's sickness had settled into her, filled her unawares, like a cancer, winged swiftly past him, like a shadow at the periphery of his vision.

Clearly the children saw it, though they never said anything. They kept their eyes on his face.

Not until Sayre ran the pearls through her teeth did he know, with a finality so shocking that it literally stopped his heart, that his love and his cowardice had cost his children their lives.

After, all he could do was shield her as she slipped deeper into delusion, into horror. He had tried, once, to bring her back, to draw her out of her agony.

"Sayre," he said gently, kneeling before her, enclosing her small, cold fists in his hands. "I am going to tell you something now that I never wanted to, that I thought I could keep...."

She cringed, her clenched fists smalling in his grasp.

"...that your father didn't want you to know. He told you that your mother was sick, but that is not entirely true, Sayre. Your father put that out—wanted people to think that. He built up this story around the truth hoping I guess that eventually the lie would grow up over the truth, kill it like a weed. Smother the talk."

Sayre began to smile. He saw it. He saw, incredibly, the deepening at the corners of her thinned lips, the crinkling of her papery flesh.

"Sayre, don't leave me." He grabbed her stick-like upper arms and shook her gently.

She had drifted to Lorelei, Lorelei glimmering in twisted deep green jungle growth, but as her spirit merged with the moon glow of Lorelei, she felt the warm, slick pelts, the meat heat of fat black rats crawling over her shoulders, down her naked breasts and she lifted her head, her eyes shut tight, and began the moaning that would grow shrill shriller...

Gerald shook her hard. Shook her eyes open. She saw him.

"Listen to me, goddamnit. *You will hear me.* Your mother was *insane*," he shouted. He paused a moment to calm himself and then continued, his voice firm but controlled. "And she knew it, so she started taking poison, a little bit at a time, hoping no one would notice, hoping they would believe that she was dying of a cancer. Your father was afraid for you, Sayre. Don't you remember the arguing behind closed doors, her fury? She was enraged that she was losing her mind, that you, her beautiful daughter, would inherit the madness. She was enraged enough to want to *kill*, Sayre." Gerald tightened his grip on Sayre's skeletal arms. "Sayre, she wanted to remove every trace of herself—including you."

Sayre was sitting calmly now, regarding Gerald curiously. Exhausted, he released her hands and slumped back on his heels. "She was insane, Sayre. So your father put her in that house with Mary and Jenny to take care of her and he went to see her nearly every day and was actually with her when she died and then he rode in the rain all the way to our place. Stood out behind the house under a tree, weeping. Mother finally saw him and went out. I never knew any of it. All I know is what Mother told me later."

"Why did he go to your mother?" Sayre said quietly.

Gerald slowly raised his head. She was back. He was afraid to move, lest he frighten her away. He barely moved his lips as he spoke.

"Our families were very close, for generations. You know that."

Sayre cocked her head slightly, puzzled as a child. Gerald's smile faltered. He had lost her. In less than the blink of an eye, she had slipped away.

"Who are you?" Sayre asked. She gazed at him with puzzled, wondering eyes.

"I am your husband Gerald. It's not your fault, Sayre. That's what I'm trying to tell you. You never had a chance. It's my fault I didn't, wouldn't see it. Didn't do anything—to protect our children..."

Clara sighed and stood up. A heavy-set, middle-aged woman tired of her baby brother's nonsense. She looked down at him. "Have you entirely lost your mind? Get up."

Gerald got up, unutterably tired. Sayre walked away toward the kitchen with the faltering steps of an old woman.

"Sayre," he said, and she turned.

"It's all my fault. No, it's, it's nobody's fault. It's not your father's fault or anybody...."

Sayre stood in the doorway of the kitchen, coolly appraising him.

"Gerry," she said calmly, and not unkindly. "I think you are losing your mind. You are a confirmed old bachelor and I am a perfectly contented old maid. Whatever children could you possibly be referring to?" Sayre turned and continued into the kitchen. "And if you want to know the truth, I thank God every day I never had any."

In her darkest dream, Sayre is lying weakly against the wall beside her broken bedroom window. She is barefooted, wearing a black dress blackened with blood, her blood seeping beneath her as he walks across the floor and sinks to his knees in the glass. Pieces of glass break under the weight of his knees and the knees of his pants turned dark. Gently he pulls Sayre's thin, limp body to him and closes his arms around her, covering her head with one hand, pressing it close against his chest, slowly rocking forward and back, forward and back until she stops breathing. Then slowly he sits down in the glass, lifting her body to cradle her in his lap. Stroking her face, her hair, gazing at the sky and tree tops through the broken window, watching the sky cool and grey as moment by moment she turns to marble in his arms.

The glass wind chimes turn, tinkling, as Gerald lifts her off the bed, he is holding her in his arms, rocking her gently as she sleeps, murmuring, "A dream, Sayre, only a dream. Nothing is broken darling." He leans and breathes in her ear. "Sayre, Sayre it is only your heart that is broken."

Sayre opened her eyes. She gazed up at Gerald in surprise, in the deep joy of awakening in her father's arms, free at last of her bad dreams.

"Father," she said.

Gerald looked down into her happy, child-like eyes.

"Sayre?" His face went cold to the bone.

"*Clar*, Daddy. Don't tease. You know I'm not Mama."

All the long, hot, smothering afternoon after the children's funeral, Gerald held Sayre until consciousness left her again, rocking, rocking, his face turned sadly to the window, to the waning light. He understood that she was gone. He knew that he had lost her.

In the gift shop below, in the room that had been the kitchen, Mrs. Dulcet turned out the last light and paused at the door before going out. She listened. Heard the floor above creaking. It was like the sound of someone shifting her weight from foot to foot. Or the sound of a rocking chair. Mrs. Dulcet smiled and went out, locking the door. Carefully descending the short flight of concrete steps to the walk, she continued on out the gate, closing it gently behind her.

A few moments later, the headlights of her car, swinging briefly across the darkened front of the Cuvier house, swept also across the wall of Gerald and Sayre's empty bedroom.

END

Made in the USA
Charleston, SC
02 October 2016